Barbie COLLECTOR'S GUIDE

CONTENTS

INTRODUCTION

Barbie may look like a doll, but she is so much more than that. Barbie began as a dream one woman had for her young daughter. Ruth Handler, an inventor and businessperson, was disappointed with the doll options her daughter, Barbara, had available to her. She noticed the toys available for girls were limiting their imaginations. What if there was a doll that showed girls they could be anything? This simple idea launched a worldwide phenomenon and the icon we know today as Barbie.

Elliot Handler, Walt Disney, and Ruth Handler

On March 9, 1959, Barbie debuted at the New York Toy Fair. While this book certainly cannot contain every single Barbie ever made since then, it highlights the journey Barbie has taken from her creation to where she is today. Are you ready to uncover some of her most iconic moments? Turn the page to get started!

ORIGINAL DOLLS

The first Barbie ever created was released on March 9, 1959. No one knew how iconic Barbie would become—in fact, some people doubted she would ever be a hit! Discover some of the first Barbie dolls that were available through the early 1960s in the next few pages. Which one is your favorite?

Barbie

FULL NAME	Barbara Millicent Roberts
CREATOR	Ruth Handler
RELEASE DATE	March 9, 1959
HEIGHT	11 inches
IGNATURE STYLE	Black-and-white strapless swimsuit and ponytail
ACCESSORIES	White sunglasses, gold hoop earrings, and black, open-toed heels
HAIR FLAIR	The very first Barbie had two hair color options, brunette and blonde.
HOMETOWN	Willows, Wisconsin

BARBIE Q

RELEASE YEAR 1959

SIGNATURE STYLE Rose-colored cotton sunback dress and white apron complete with multiple pockets

ACCESSORIES Chef's hat, white heels, rolling pin, spatula, spoon, knife, and potholder

Who's Hungry?

Barbie is ready to cook up a storm in this outfit.

EASTER PARADE

RELEASE YEAR 1959

SIGNATURE STYLE Silk taffeta flare coat with polished cotton apple print sheath dress

ACCESSORIES Pearl earrings and necklace, black bow headband, plastic patent leather clutch bag, white gloves, and black heels

Parade Pride

Barbie would look elegant wearing this dress at any parade.

COMMUTER SET™

RELEASE YEAR 1959

SIGNATURE STYLE Two-piece suit with light blue checked shirt

ACCESSORIES White gloves, crystal rope beaded necklace and bracelet, black shoes, red petal cloche hat, and red hatbox

Cool Commute

The red hatbox was the perfect size for carrying hats or anything else Barbie needed.

GAY PARISIENNE™

RELEASE YEAR 1959

SIGNATURE STYLE Strapless nylon taffeta dress with pin-dot pattern

ACCESSORIES White fur stole, headband hat with tulle veil, pearl necklace and earrings, and gold velvet purse

Très Chic

This glamorous look was the top fashion news of Paris!

ROMAN HOLIDAY

RELEASE YEAR 1959

SIGNATURE STYLE Scoop neck red-striped top with navy blue sheath skirt and rib-striped travel coat

ACCESSORIES Straw half-hat, pearl necklace, white gloves, red shoes, white purse, and red glasses

Happy Holiday

Stripes on stripes never looked so good

PICNIC SET™

RELEASE YEAR 1959

SIGNATURE STYLE Red gingham shirt with dark denim jeans

ACCESSORIES Straw hat, wedge shoes, fishing pole, and picnic basket

Gone Fishin'

A picnic basket may be an unusual item to carry fish in, but it works for Barbie!

SUBURBAN SHOPPER™

RELEASE YEAR 1959

SIGNATURE STYLE Blue-and-white striped sundress made of cotton and lace

ACCESSORIES Cartwheel straw hat, blue rotary telephone, and tote bag filled with fruit

Out and About

This Barbie can keep cool while shopping in the summer heat thanks to her wide-brimmed straw hat.

WEDDING DAY SET

RELEASE YEAR 1959

SIGNATURE STYLE Elegant white satin wedding gown with billowing layers of flowered nylon tulle and formal train

ACCESSORIES White nylon gloves, bridal bouquet, and white shoes

Fit for a Queen

White wedding gowns became popular in 1840 thanks to Queen Victoria.

ENCHANTED EVENING

RELEASE YEAR 1960

SIGNATURE STYLE Pink satin floor-length gown with flowing train

ACCESSORIES Pearl necklace and drop earrings, pink heels with silver glitter, elbow-length gloves, and white fur stole

Satin Sophistication

This formal gown would be perfect for any elegant affair.

SOLO IN THE SPOTLIGHT

RELEASE YEAR 1960

SIGNATURE STYLE Dramatic black strapless glitter gown with rose detailing

ACCESSORIES Long black nylon gloves, pink scarf, bead necklace, black heels, and microphone

Soprano Star

Onstage, this Barbie always sings her heart out.

OPEN ROAD

RELEASE YEAR	1961
SIGNATURE STYLE	Beige sweater, striped pants, and car coat fastened with toggles
ACCESSORIES	Straw hat with red scarf tie, wedge sandals, and map

Road Trip

Whatever road she takes, Barbie is always up for an adventure!

SHEATH SENSATION

RELEASE YEAR	1961
SIGNATURE STYLE	Red cotton sheath dress with four gold buttons and two pockets
ACCESSORIES	Crisp white straw hat, short white gloves, and white heels

Fashion History

The sheath dress dates all the way back to ancient Egyptian times!

FRIDAY NIGHT DATE

RELEASE YEAR 1960

SIGNATURE STYLE Powder blue corduroy jumper with colorful felt appliqués, white blouse, and bouffant pettiskirt

ACCESSORIES Black tray and two plastic tumbler glasses with drinking straws

Order Up

If Barbie drops her beverage tray, the glasses won't spill. That's because the orange "liquid" inside isn't real.

RED FLARE

RELEASE YEAR 1960

SIGNATURE STYLE Red velvet flared coat with bell sleeves and white satin lining

ACCESSORIES Red pillbox hat, handbag, white gloves, and red shoes

Fashion History

Velvet is historically made from silk fabric.

BLACK MAGIC

RELEASE YEAR 1964

SIGNATURE STYLE Black sheath dress with black tulle cape

ACCESSORIES Black gloves, black heels, and gold purse

Delightfully Daring

Black casts a spell with this chic evening look.

THEATRE DATE

RELEASE YEAR 1964

SIGNATURE STYLE Emerald green satin suit with peplum skirt and white satin blouse

ACCESSORIES Emerald green satin hat and green shoes

Out on the Town

Barbie could wear this look to the theater or to dinner at a nice restaurant.

WORLD of BARBIE

Barbie has experienced many changes since the early 1960s. For example, from her first family to her first friends, only two remain the same—Ken and Skipper. Learn more facts about her friends and family then and now in the following pages.

Barbie

FULL NAME	Ken
RELEASE YEAR	1961
HEIGHT	12 inches
SIGNATURE STYLE	Red swim trunks, striped beach jacket, and sandals

First Friend

Ken was the very first friend Barbie ever made!

RIENDS: Then

vo years after Barbie was
leased, she got her first
iend, Ken! Since then, she's
ade a ton of friends with all
nds of personalities.

MIDGE HADLEY

RELEASE YEAR 1963

GNATURE STYLE Red bathing suit and heels

Friendly Face

Midge had freckles!

CHRISTIE

RELEASE YEAR 1968

SIGNATURE STYLE Neon-colored top and orange shorts

Talk of the Town

Christie was first released as Talking Christie—a doll that could talk!

KEN CARSON

LIKES The beach, surfing, sailing, and marine science

#1 Dream

Being a lifeguard when he turns 18

RENEE CHAO

LIKES Sports, sports, and more sports

FEARS Being trapped in a small space

NICOLE "NIKKI" WATKINS

MOTTO
"Why be them when you can be you?"

Future Career
Entrepreneur or politician

TERESA RIVERA

KES
earning something ew, movies, and anging out with er friends

Most Likely To
Invent something

DAISY KOSTOPOULOS

LIKES
Music—anything that brings people together (especially if there's a turntable involved)

Most Likely To
Drop a beat

FAMILY: Then

In the 1960s, the Roberts family looked pretty different from how it looks today! Only one family member has remained the same—Skipper! Did you know Barbie used to have twin siblings? Learn more about the Roberts family from the 1960s here.

TUTTI AND TODD

RELEASE YEAR 1965

Twin Trivia

Preschool-aged twins Tutti and Todd were the youngest siblings. They liked to build sandcastles and play in puddles.

SKIPPER

RELEASE YEAR 1964

Solo Sister

Skipper was the first sibling of Barbie ever released.

FRANCIE

RELEASE YEAR 1966

Mad for Mod

Cousin Francie had a mod fashion sense that was very on trend for her time period.

With Barbie and her three younger sisters, the Roberts family has a full Dreamhouse (not to mention their four puppies and Blissa the cat). One thing is for sure—with so many different personalities, every day is an adventure.

CHELSEA

AGE 6

DISLIKES Being treated like a little kid

All About Chelsea

She's a prankster who is creative and imaginative. She loves all creatures, real or imaginary.

SKIPPER

AGE 14½

LIKES All things tech

DISLIKES When her phone dies, being pranked

STACIE

AGE 10

LIKES Sports, competitions, challenges, anything that gets her blood pumping

Motto

"Sometimes the shortest distance between two points is straight through the wall."

DJ

LIKES Anything that involves music: dancing, howling, and moving to the beat

TALENTED TAIL-WAGGER Can howl on key

Puppy Thoughts

"My howl will be the next big thing!"

HONEY

LIKES Playing dress-up, discovering something new

POSITIVE PUP Honey always sees the bright side of things

Puppy Thoughts

"I got it right—yay me!"

BLISSA THE CAT

LIKES Napping, eating, eating more, napping again, and being pampered

DISLIKES Water, bugs, snakes, dry crunchy cat food, pet sitters, and being woken up from a nap

Kitten Thoughts

"Does that involve water? No, thanks."

ROOKIE

LIKES Physical activities like running, jumping, flipping, and pouncing

DISLIKES Having to sit still

Puppy Thoughts

"I bet I can dig the fastest!"

TAFFY

LIKES Snuggles

DISLIKES Scary situations

Puppy Thoughts

"I am *not* a scaredy dog!"

WELCOME HOME, Barbie!

Barbie moved into her very first Dreamhouse in 1962. It was a simple home, with only enough room for Barbie. It was decorated a mid-century modern style.

he Dreamhouse came with furniture, books, a television, pillows, nd other accessories. All of the furniture was made from ardboard sheets that had to be punched out and folded. The ront door was black, and the house was painted robin's-egg blue.

DREAMHOUSE

RELEASE YEAR 1962

FUN FACT The first Dreamhouse did not have a roof!

DREAMHOUSE BY THE Decade!

The Dreamhouse has certainly changed a lot through the decades. Look at these versions to see how the Dreamhouse has evolved from a one-room studio in the 1960s to the multilevel mansion it is today.

1970s

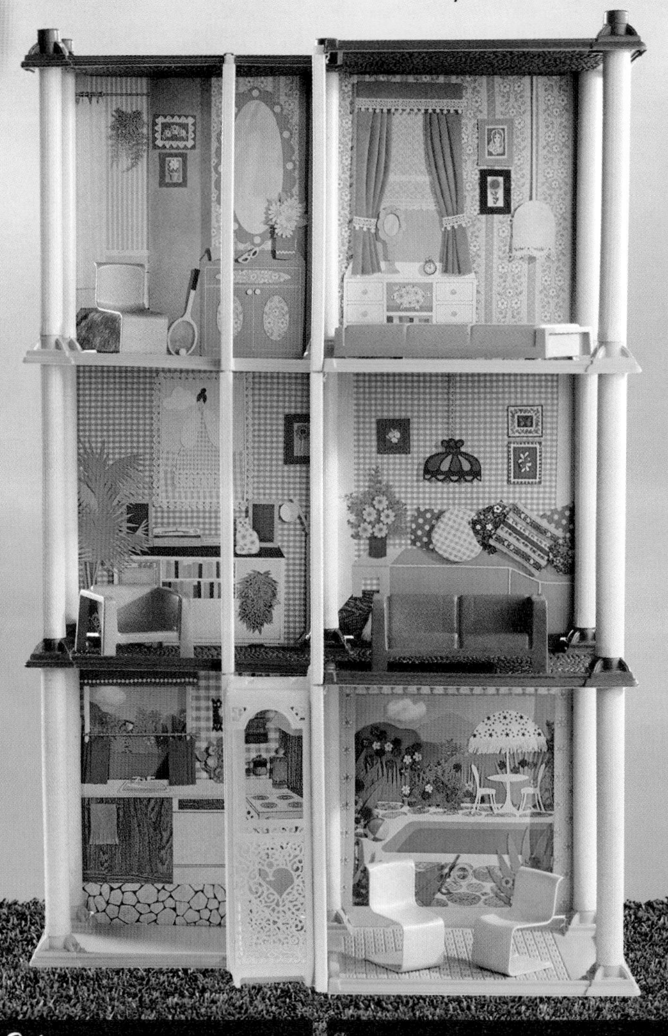

Barbie

STYLE Townhouse

RELEASE YEAR 1974

COLOR SCHEME Bright pops of color throughout, like green, orange, and pink

Elevated Look

This was the first Barbie Dreamhouse with a working elevator!

STYLE A-frame house with six rooms

RELEASE YEAR 1979, but it continued through the 1980s

COLOR SCHEME This Dreamhouse was available in white, pink, and yellow.

Home Sweet Home

This was the first Dreamhouse with working doors and windows. It also had shutters and flower planters.

MAGICAL MANSION

RELEASE YEAR 1990

STYLE Sparkly exterior with columns

COLOR SCHEME Pink, pink, and more pink!

Pretty in Pink

This was the first Dreamhouse with lights that really worked!

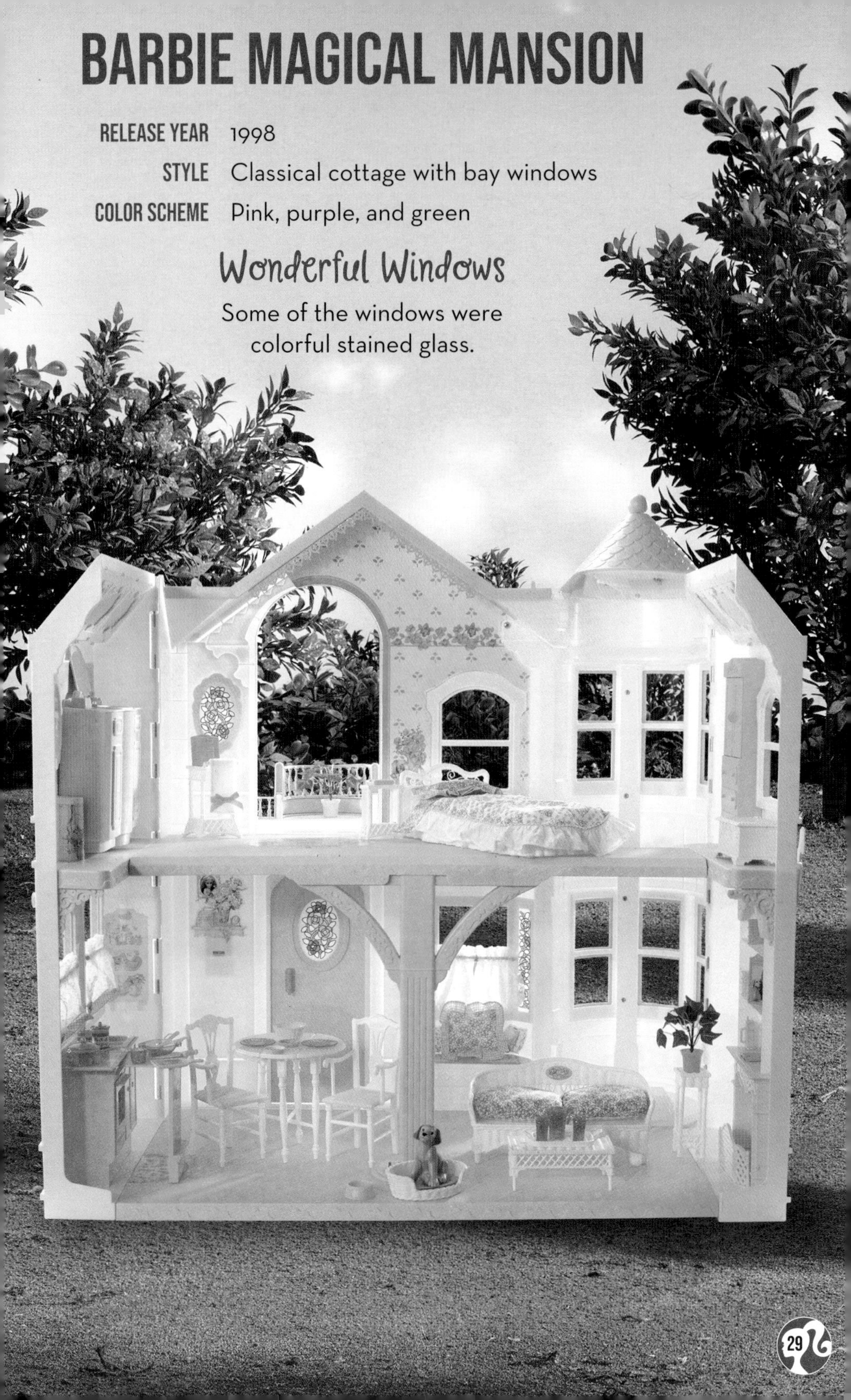

BARBIE MAGICAL MANSION

RELEASE YEAR 1998

STYLE Classical cottage with bay windows

COLOR SCHEME Pink, purple, and green

Wonderful Windows

Some of the windows were colorful stained glass.

TODAY'S DREAMHOUSE

On the other side of this office desk is a cozy fireplace, perfect for chilly nights!

If Barbie wants to host a sleepover, she can make extra room with her purple couch that converts into bunk beds.

In the kitchen, there's lots to see and hear—a sizzling frying pan, a whistling teakettle, and a light-up oven.

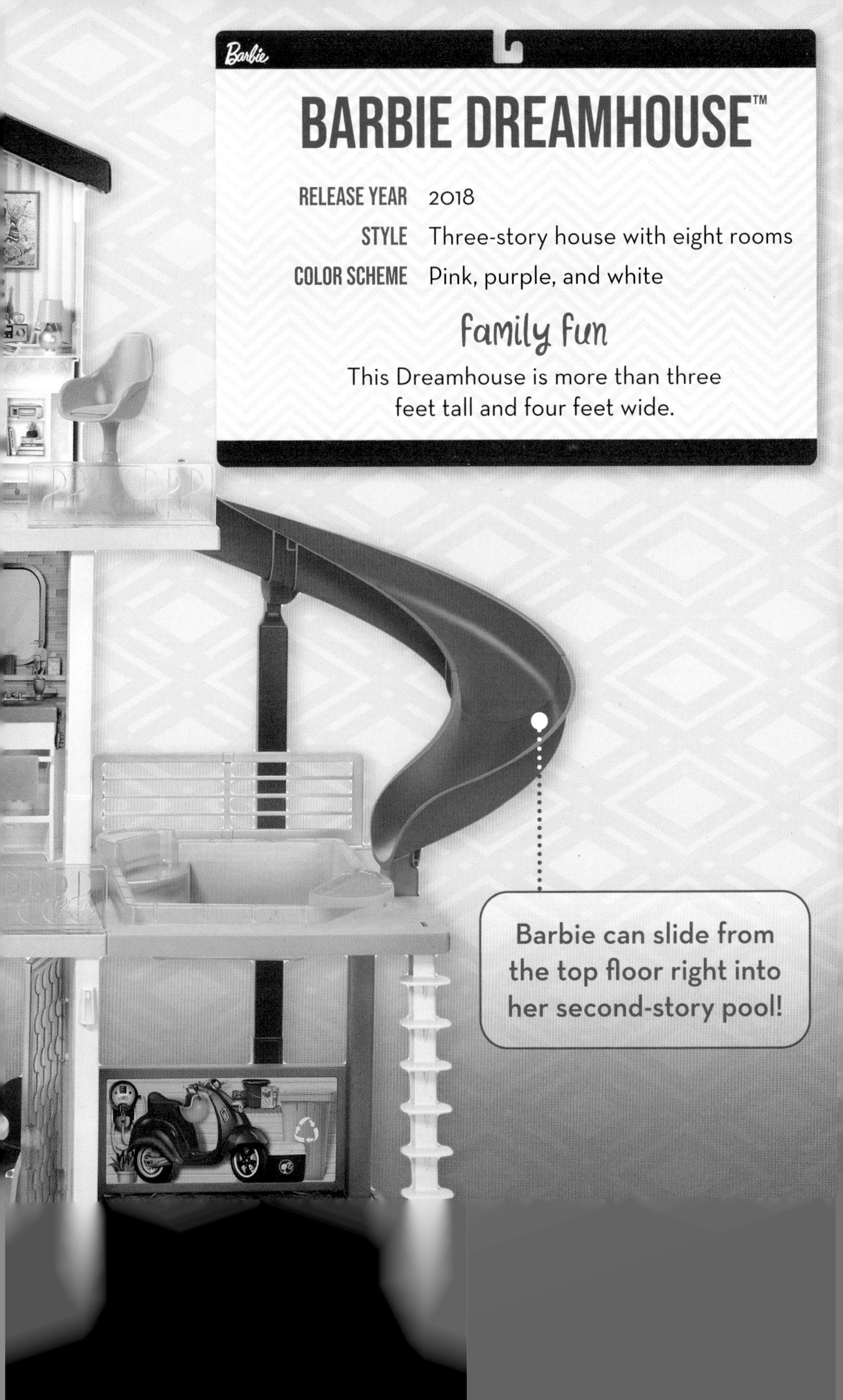
Barbie
BARBIE DREAMHOUSE™
RELEASE YEAR 2018
STYLE Three-story house with eight rooms
COLOR SCHEME Pink, purple, and white
Family Fun
This Dreamhouse is more than three feet tall and four feet wide.
Barbie can slide from the top floor right into her second-story pool!

CARS, PLANES, *and* . . . BEACH BUSES!

Barbie got her first car the same year she moved into her Dreamhouse in 1962. Today, Barbie has almost every vehicle imaginable. Check out the next few pages to see some of her vehicles throughout history.

AUSTIN-HEALEY

RELEASE YEAR 1962

Rockin' Ride

This two-seater convertible with blue seats and a peach exterior was the first car Barbie ever had.

STAR 'VETTE

RELEASE YEAR 1977

Star Car

This convertible was made for a star—Superstar™ Barbie!

BARBIE CONVERTIBLE

RELEASE YEAR 2020

Classic Convertible

Barbie is still rocking a two-seater convertible, similar to the very first one she owned!

SWEET ORCHARD FARM™ PICKUP TRUCK

RELEASE YEAR 2020

Tough Truck

Whether she's going to the farmers' market or to the cornfields, this truck helps Barbie get all of her jobs done.

BEACH BUS

RELEASE YEAR 1974

Playful Plates

The license plate on this bus said "SURFER

STAR TRAVELER™ MOTOR HOME

RELEASE YEAR 1982

Out of This World

This vehicle really was a home on wheels with bunk beds, a shower, a kitchen, and an area for a picnic!

DREAMPLANE™

RELEASE YEAR 2020

Fancy Flight

With a snack cart and reclining chairs, this plane really is a dream. The first Barbie airplane was released in the early 1970s.

SCOOTER

RELEASE YEAR 2020

Puppy Passenger

The blue basket on the back of this moped is perfect for Taffy to come along for a ride.

FIRST CAREERS

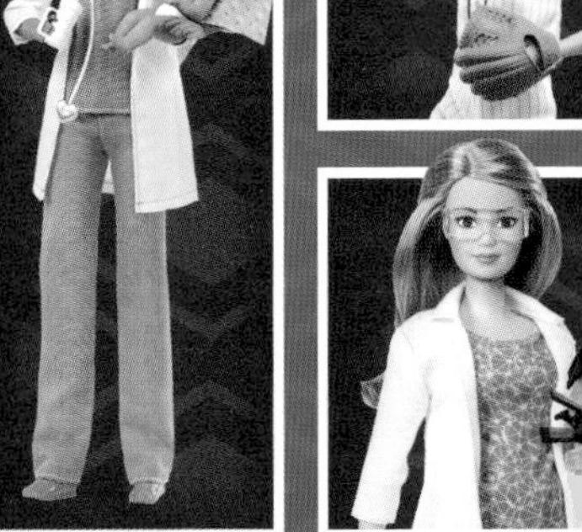

FASHION EDITOR

RELEASE YEAR 1960

SIGNATURE STYLE Red skirt with matching jacket and striped shirt

ACCESSORIES Black belt, black glasses, gold earrings, and black fashion designer portfolio

Fashion Fun

The fashion designer portfolio is the perfect place for storing designs created by Barbie.

rom aviator to zoologist, Barbie has had over 200 careers so far, nd every year she continues to explore new ones! Discover them l, from her very first career to her current occupation.

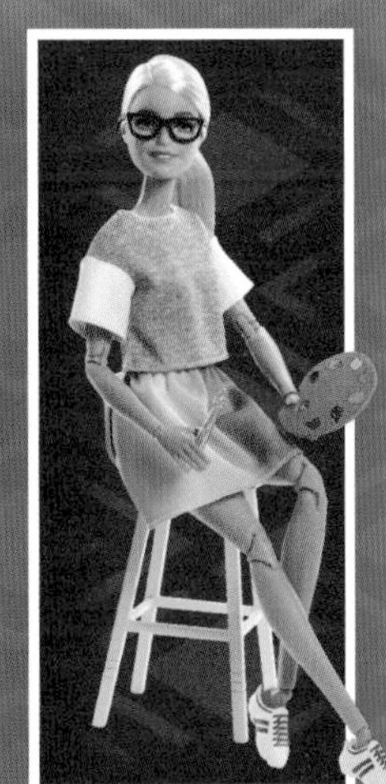

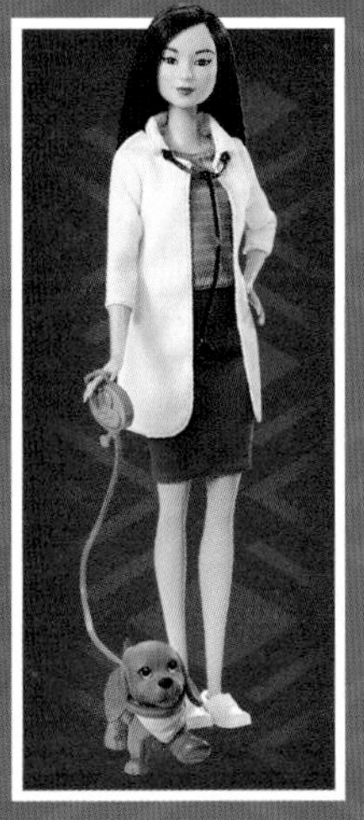

FLIGHT ATTENDANT

RELEASE YEAR 1961

SIGNATURE STYLE Blue uniform and matching blue cap

ACCESSORIES Travel bag

Ready for Takeoff

As a flight attendant, Barbie traveled the world!

REGISTERED NURSE

RELEASE YEAR 1961

SIGNATURE STYLE White cotton uniform and navy blue cape lined with red silk

ACCESSORIES Hot water bottle, diploma, medicine bottle, spoon, and black eyeglasses

Helping Hand

From the beginning, Barbie liked to help people, which made this career one of her favorites.

Diploma
#991
REGISTERED NURSE
(without doll) #991
Barbie cures patients in a trim white cotton uniform with zipper back, buttoned blouse and real hip pockets. With her spectacles and graduate nurse's cap, she wears a navy blue cape lined in red silk for outside calls. Hot water bottle, diploma, medicine bottle and spoon complete the set. $3.00

EXECUTIVE CAREER GIRL

RELEASE YEAR	1963
SIGNATURE STYLE	White-and-black tweed suit with skirt
ACCESSORIES	Cloche hat with rose detailing, long black gloves, and black heels

Girl Power

Being an executive career girl put the emphasis on success for Barbie.

Barbie has always been inspired by astronauts who accomplish amazing things! Check out her different space looks and learn about her favorite space *she*roes here. That's one small step for Barbie, one giant leap for humankind!

1960s

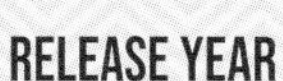

Barbie

RELEASE YEAR
1965

SIGNATURE STYLE
Silver metallic space suit with brown detailing

ACCESSORIES
Brown mittens with matching boots and white space helmet

SPACE STATS
Two years before Barbie went to space, Valentina Tereshkova became the first woman in space.

1980s

Barbie

RELEASE YEAR
1985

SIGNATURE STYLE
Metallic pink space suit with silver top

ACCESSORIES
Pink knee-high boots, silver belt, and helmet

SPACE STATS
In 1983, Sally Ride became the first American woman to go to space.

1990s

RELEASE YEAR
2013

SIGNATURE STYLE
White astronaut suit with pink detailing

ACCESSORIES
Pink helmet, pink boots, and pink space pack

SPACE STATS
Outside of a spacecraft, astronauts need to wear a helmet so they can breathe.

2010s

RELEASE YEAR
1994

SIGNATURE STYLE
White space suit with red and silver detailing and silver boots

ACCESSORIES
Barbie flag, helmet, space accessories, and glow-in-the-dark moon rocks

SPACE STATS
In 1992, Mae Jemison became the first Black woman to travel to space.

RELEASE YEAR
2019

SIGNATURE STYLE
White astronaut suit with blue and pink detailing

ACCESSORIES
White helmet, gloves, and boots

SPACE STATS
The first women-only spacewalk took place in 2019 with Jessica Meir and Christina Koch.

CAREERS: 1970s and 1980s

SURGEON

RELEASE YEAR 1973

SIGNATURE STYLE Blue scrubs with matching hair covering, surgical mask, and stethoscope

ACCESSORIES Surgical mask and cap, stethoscope, and towel

Steady Hands

To become a surgeon, Barbie had to go to school for more than 10 years.

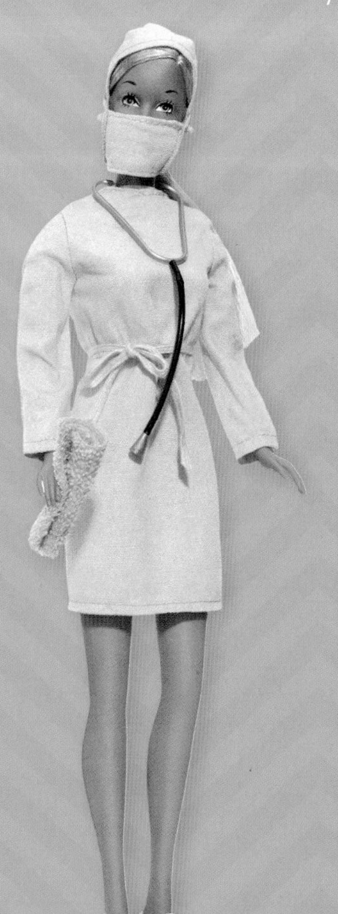

AEROBICS INSTRUCTOR

RELEASE YEAR 1984

SIGNATURE STYLE Leotard, striped legwarmers, and headband

ACCESSORIES Workout bag, pink sash, ballet slippers, and exercise book

Work It Out

Aerobics was a very popular workou trend in the 1980s that involved dancing and stretching.

VETERINARIAN

RELEASE YEAR

1985

SIGNATURE STYLE

White doctor's coat, pink pants with paw print pattern, and stethoscope

Not Just Dogs

Veterinarians treat all different types of animals, including snakes, horses, and more.

CEO

RELEASE YEAR

1985

SIGNATURE STYLE

Pink power suit with matching white-and-pink hat and briefcase

Another Name

This Barbie is also called Day-to-Night™ Barbie.

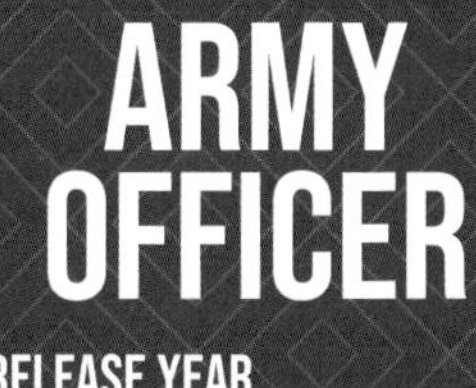

ARMY OFFICER

RELEASE YEAR

1989

SIGNATURE STYLE

Jacket with gold detailing and matching skirt

Take Charge

This was the first position with the U.S. military that Barbie held. Since then, she has enlisted in the Marines, Air Force, and Navy.

PILOT

RELEASE YEAR

1989

SIGNATURE STYLE

Pink pilot uniform, pink pilot cap, and pink shoes

Sky High

Pilots fly planes over 30,000 feet in the air.

POLICE OFFICER

RELEASE YEAR

1993

SIGNATURE STYLE

Dark blue police officer uniform, hat, and belt

Safety First

Police Officer Barbie has some safety tips that include: "Always wear your seat belt" and "Look both ways before you cross the street."

ARMY MEDIC

RELEASE YEAR

1993

SIGNATURE STYLE

Camouflage uniform, two army medic bags, and maroon beret with army medic symbol on the front

Military Medic

Barbie was a sergeant in the 101st Airborne Division.

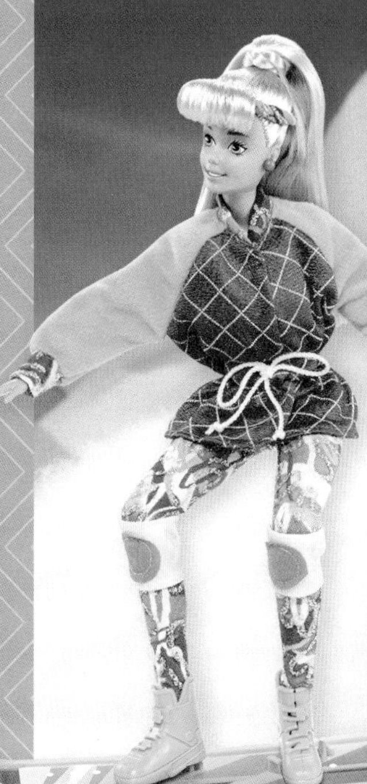

SNOWBOARD

RELEASE YEAR

1995

SIGNATURE STYLE

Pink, yellow, and blue winter jacket with yellow tie and rainbow-colored pants

Ice, Ice, Barbi

This Barbie did more than just snowboarding—she a had skis and skates

IREFIGHTER

LEASE YEAR

95

NATURE STYLE

llow turnout coat, oots, and helmet

Hot Dog

his Barbie came with a Dalmatian firedog.

PALEONTOLOGIST

RELEASE YEAR

1997

SIGNATURE STYLE

Dinosaur print button-down shirt, tan shorts, and pink neck scarf

What's in a Name?

The word "dinosaur" means "terrible lizard."

SOCCER PLAYER

RELEASE YEAR

1999

SIGNATURE STYLE

Red, white, and blue soccer uniform, black cleats, and white shin guards

Kickin' It

In 1991, Team USA won the first Women's World Cup tournament.

BARBIE FOR PRESIDENT!

Barbie has run for president of the United States every election year since 1992, except for one. In 2016, she made *her*story with the first all-female ticket.

RELEASE YEAR

1992

SIGNATURE STYLE

This Barbie came with two outfits—a stars and stripes–themed ball gown with a silver top, and a red skirt suit with gold trim and a white top.

Madam President

This was the first time Barbie ran for president.

RELEASE YEAR

2000

SIGNATURE STYLE

Blue power suit and blue shoes

First First Lady

In 2000, Hillary Clinton was elected to the U.S. Senate. It was the first time a former First Lady was elected to public office.

RELEASE YEAR

2004

SIGNATURE STYLE

Red pant suit and stars and stripes sca

Power Move

In 2005, Condoleez
Rice became Secretary of State, making her the first Black woman to hol
the position.

LEASE YEAR
008

GNATURE STYLE
lue pinstriped suit
ith glitter details
nd pink top with
ark pink dots

Presidential Pioneer

In 1872, Victoria Woodhull became the first woman residential candidate in the U.S., paving the way for future generations.

RELEASE YEAR
2012

SIGNATURE STYLE
Pink suit with skirt and light pink top

Golden Age

To be president, a candidate must be at least 35 years old.

RELEASE YEAR
2016

SIGNATURE STYLE
Red-and-white jacket with black lining and blue pencil skirt

That's the Ticket

This was the first time Barbie had a running mate.

SIGN LANGUAGE TEACHER BARBIE

RELEASE YEAR 2001

SIGNATURE STYLE Light blue knit shirt, matching cardigan, and short plaid skirt

Sure Sign

This Barbie is making the American Sign Language sign for "I love you."

AVIATOR BARBIE

RELEASE YEAR

2002

SIGNATURE STYLE

Olive green flight suit and jacke and white helmet.

Sky's the Limit

Amelia Earhart, Bessie Colemar and Willa Brown are some of th most famous female aviators.

TEACHER

RELEASE YEAR 2002

SIGNATURE STYLE Yellow shirt with red belt, patterned skirt, and pink polka dot scarf

Love of Learning

Barbie has been in the field of education since she started as a student teacher in 1965.

ZOOLOGIST

RELEASE YEAR 2006

SIGNATURE STYLE Khaki shorts and short-sleeve top with paw print patch

All About Animals

Zoologists study everything about animals—where they live, how they act, and how humans interact with them.

SPORTS: 2010s

Whether she's driving at top speed around a racetrack or competing in a worldwide gymnastics competition, Barbie gives it her all. Check out these cool careers Barbie has held in the field of sports.

RACE CAR DRIVER

RELEASE YEAR

2010

Take the Wheel

When a race car pulls over for gas or other services during a race, it's called a pit stop.

RIBBON GYMNAST

RELEASE YEAR

2016

Ribbon Rhythms

Some of the moves a ribbon gymnast uses are called snakes, tosses, and spirals.

MARTIAL ARTIST

RELEASE YEAR

2016

Did You Know

The first woman tc become a 10th-leve black belt (which is the highest level) wa 98 years old!

KATEBOARDER

LEASE YEAR

017

The first female professional skateboarder was Patti McGee.

ROCK CLIMBER

RELEASE YEAR

2017

That Rocks

When a rock climber climbs down a cliff, it's called rappelling.

BASEBALL PLAYER

RELEASE YEAR

2018

Lucky Number 13

There are 13 different types of pitches that a pitcher can throw.

ICE SKATER

RELEASE YEAR

2017

What's in a Name?

Jumps like the Axel, Lutz, and Salchow are named after the people who created them.

TENNIS PLAYER

RELEASE YEAR

2017

Love the Game

When it comes to tennis scores, the word "love" means zero.

GYMNASTICS COACH

RELEASE YEAR

2018

Caring Coach

A gymnastics coach helps gymnasts work on the skills they nee to perform their best

SOCCER PLAYER

RELEASE YEAR

2018

What's in a Name?

In the United Kingdom, soccer is called football.

BASKETBALL PLAYER

RELEASE YEAR

2019

Basketball Beginnings

The first basketball game ever played occurred in 1891 in Springfield, Massachusetts.

BOXER

RELEASE YEAR

2020

First Match

The first U.S. women's boxing match was held in New York City in 1876.

MUSIC & THE ARTS

Whether Barbie performs for a huge crowd or just for herself, she gives it her all. Writing music, developing her own dance routines, and teaching others how to express themselves through music are some of her favorite activities. In this section, discover some of Barbie's recent careers in music and the arts.

FILM DIRECTOR

RELEASE YEAR

2015

Silver Screen

A film director takes a script and works with a crew to bring it to the silver screen.

BALLERINA

RELEASE YEAR

2016

Did You Know

The first Black principal dancer for the American Ballet Theatre was Misty Copeland.

MUSICIAN

RELEASE YEAR

2017

Play It by Ear

Musicians play all different types of instruments, but the oldest one is a flute.

POP STAR

RELEASE YEAR 2018

Record Sales

If a pop star has a platinum album, it means it sold more than a million copies.

MUSIC TEACHER

RELEASE YEAR

2019

Knowledge Is Power

A woman named Julia Crane opened the first school for music educators in the U.S. in 1896.

CARING FOR OTHERS

Caring for others has always been a priority for Barbie. She has been in the business of helping others since she became a registered nurse in 1961. Since then, she's branched out into many other areas of service. Check out some of those careers here!

LIFEGUARD

RELEASE YEAR 2015

Water, Water Everywhere

Lifeguards can supervise swimmers in a pool, beach, lake, or any other body of water.

NURSE

RELEASE YEAR 2016

Did You Know?

There are three times as many nurses in the U.S. than doctors.

EYE DOCTOR

RELEASE YEAR 2016

What's in a Name?

The chart that an eye doctor asks a patient to read to check their vision is called a Snellen chart.

DOCTOR

RELEASE YEAR 2018

Foot Focus

A doctor that specializes in foot and ankle problems is called a podiatrist.

VETERINARIAN

RELEASE YEAR 2016

Did You Know

There are currently more female veterinarians than male veterinarians in the U.S.

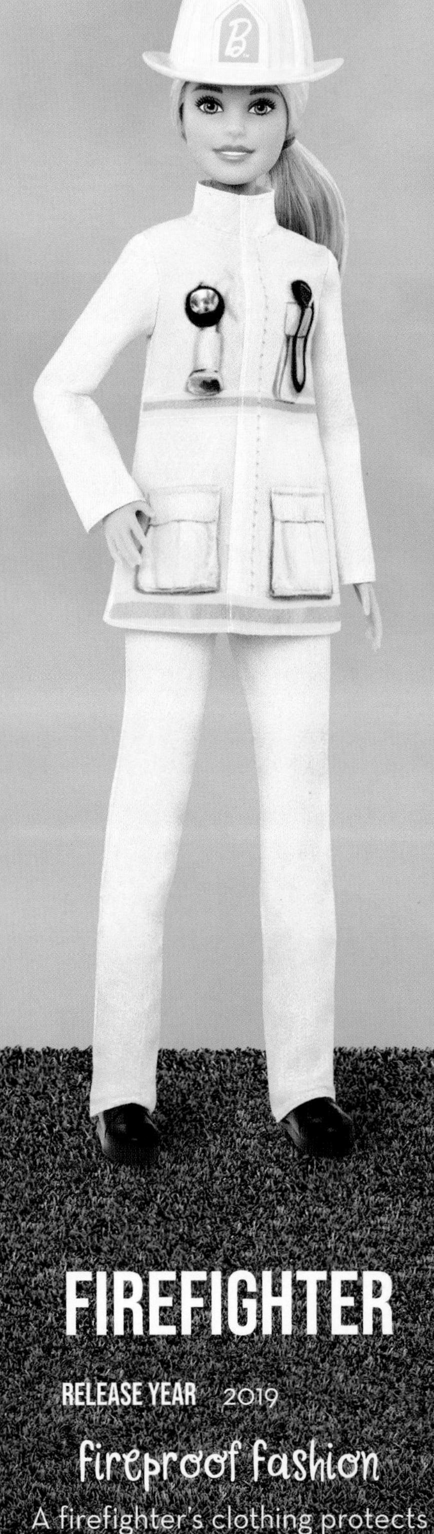

FIREFIGHTER

RELEASE YEAR 2019

Fireproof Fashion

A firefighter's clothing protects them from the hot flames when they're putting out a fire.

BABY DOCTOR

RELEASE YEAR

2019

What's in a Name?

A doctor who specializes in caring for babies is called a pediatrician.

DENTIST

RELEASE YEAR

2019

Say Cheese

A dentist helps keep their patients' teeth and gums healthy, and their smile bright.

JUDGE

RELEASE YEAR

2019

Barrier Breaker

In 1981, Sandra Day O'Connor became the first woman to serve as a justice on the Supreme Court.

AROUND TOWN

Positively impacting her community is super important to Barbie. Whether she is helping bui a new community center or is selling fruits and vegetables at her local farmers' market, Barbie likes being an important part of her town. Look at some of the careers Barbie has had that have directly impacted her community.

ARCHITECT

RELEASE YEAR

2011

Making Plans

An architect designs the plans to make a building.

DETECTIVE

RELEASE YEAR

2014

Crime Solver

Clues like fingerprints and witness statements help a detective solve a crime.

BUILDER

RELEASE YEAR

2017

Construction Crew

A builder takes an architect's plans and builds the building with a crew.

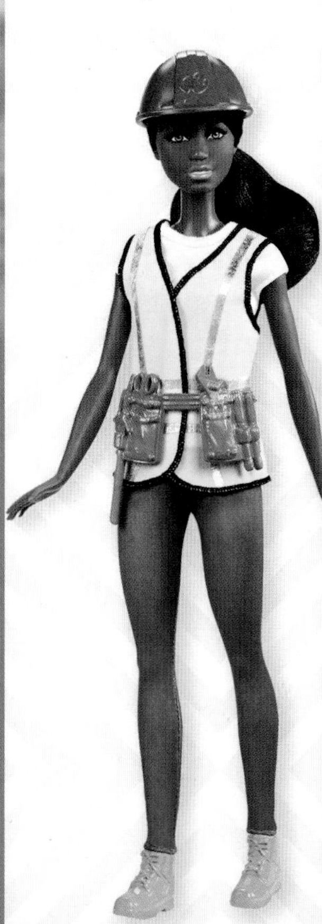

FARMER

RELEASE YEAR

2018

Did You Know?

Farmers can grow crops like fruits and vegetables, or take care of animals like chickens and cows.

BEEKEEPER

RELEASE YEAR

2018

What's in a Name?

Another word for beekeeper is apiarist.

NEWS ANCHOR

RELEASE YEAR

2019

Famous Faces

Diane Sawyer, Ann Curry, and Hoda Kotb are all successful news anchors.

CULINARY ARTS

Barbie loves bringing her family and friends together around a meal that she has poured her heart into. Cooking and baking are fun ways to show others that you care! Here are some recent careers that Barbie has held in the culinary arts.

BAKER

RELEASE YEAR 2018

So Sweet

A baker specializes in making bread and sweet treats like pies, brownies, and cakes.

CUPCAKE CHEF

RELEASE YEAR 2016

Cupcake Clay

Fondant is a type of icing used by cupcake chefs that can be molded like clay.

NOODLE MAKER

RELEASE YEAR 2019

Noodle Knowledge

Chopsticks were originally used as a cooking tool, not a utensil.

HEAD CHEF

RELEASE YEAR 2020

Did You Know?

The tall white hat that a chef wears is called a toque blanche.

SCIENCE & TECH

From digging up dinosaur bones to developing the latest game, careers in science and tech are so cool! Explore some of the careers Barbie has held in these fields—you'll never know what you may *dig* up!

Barbie
COMPUTER ENGINEER
RELEASE YEAR 2011
Teeny-Tiny
A single grain of rice is larger than the smallest computer in the world.
Barbie
SCIENTIST
RELEASE YEAR 2016
DNA Discovery
Rosalind Franklin was one of the scientists who helped our understanding of DNA by discovering its density and spiral shape.

Barbie

GAME DEVELOPER

RELEASE YEAR 2016

Big Ideas

A game developer takes an idea for a video game, computer game, or app and turns it into a real game!

Barbie

ROBOTICS ENGINEER

RELEASE YEAR 2018

Dancing Robots

Some robotics engineers program robots to perform specific tasks.

Barbie

PALEONTOLOGIST

RELEASE YEAR 2017

Did You Know?

A woman named Mary Anning was one of the first paleontologists. She discovered her first major fossil when she was 12 years old.

MAJOR MOMENTS

From a solid piece of plastic in 1959 to today's Made to Move™ Barbie that has 22 "joints," Barbie has experienced a lot of makeovers in the more than 60 years she has existed. In this section, discover some of her most significant moments that led her to becoming the doll she is today.

MAJOR MOMENTS: 1960s

lot changed for Barbie in
er first decade—she met her
iends, family, and moved into her very first Dreamhouse. But her look,
om her hair to the way her body moved, also changed quite a bit during
is time. Check out these major moments from the 1960s.

FASHION QUEEN

RELEASE YEAR 1963

GNATURE STYLE Strapless swimsuit with white and gold stripes and matching hair scarf

fun fact

'his Barbie had brown sculpted hair and three wigs so she could match her hair with her fashion.

MISS BARBIE

RELEASE YEAR 1964

SIGNATURE STYLE Pink swimsuit with gold dots and pink swim cap with fringe

fun fact

This was the first Barbie doll whose eyelids could close.

Barbie

BENDABLE LEG BARBIE

RELEASE YEAR 1965

SIGNATURE STYLE Swimsuit with multicolored striped top and solid blue bottom

fun fact

This was the first Barbie whose legs could bend.

Barbie
TWIST 'N' TURN™
RELEASE YEAR 1967
SIGNATURE STYLE Mesh cover-up with orange two-piece swimsuit
fun fact
For the first time, Barbie could twist from her torso.
JUST AS EASY AS
1 TAKE YOUR OLD DOLL TO THE NEAREST TOY STORE
2 ALONG WITH $1.50
3 AND TRADE HER FOR THE NEW TWIST 'N' TURN BARBIE
TO OWN THE NEW TWIST 'N' TURN BARBIE

MAJOR MOMENTS: 1970s

The 1970s brought more changes with Living Barbie an Live Action Barbie, both of which allowed Barbie to move in new ways. Malibu Barbie and Superstar Barbie were some of the most iconic dolls from that decade, solidifying her reputation as a Malibu beach–loving gal and a superstar with a smile.

LIVE ACTION BARBIE

RELEASE YEAR 1971

SIGNATURE STYLE Graphic patterned jumpsuit with tassel on the wrists

fun fact

This Barbie came with a touch 'n' g stand that made it easier for her t show off her dance moves.

LIVING BARBIE

RELEASE YEAR 1970

SIGNATURE STYLE Silver-and-gold metallic swimsuit with mesh jacket

fun fact

For the first time, Barbie could pose like she was walking, bending, waving, or carrying something, thanks to her feet and hands being able to move.

MALIBU BARBIE

RELEASE YEAR 1971

SIGNATURE STYLE Light blue one-piece swimsuit and pink sunglasses

fun fact

Malibu Barbie had a smile with teeth for the first time and her eyes looked forward rather than to the side.

SUPERSTAR BARBIE

RELEASE YEAR 1977

SIGNATURE STYLE Hot pink satin floor-length dress with matching boa

fun fact

Superstar Barbie had a new face sculpted with a glamorous smile.

MAJOR MOMENTS: 1980s

The most iconic Barbie moment from the 1980s occurred in 1986 with the debut of Barbie and the Rockers. With big hair and even bigger musical hits, Barbie and the band captured the decade through their style and love for music. Learn about each band member here!

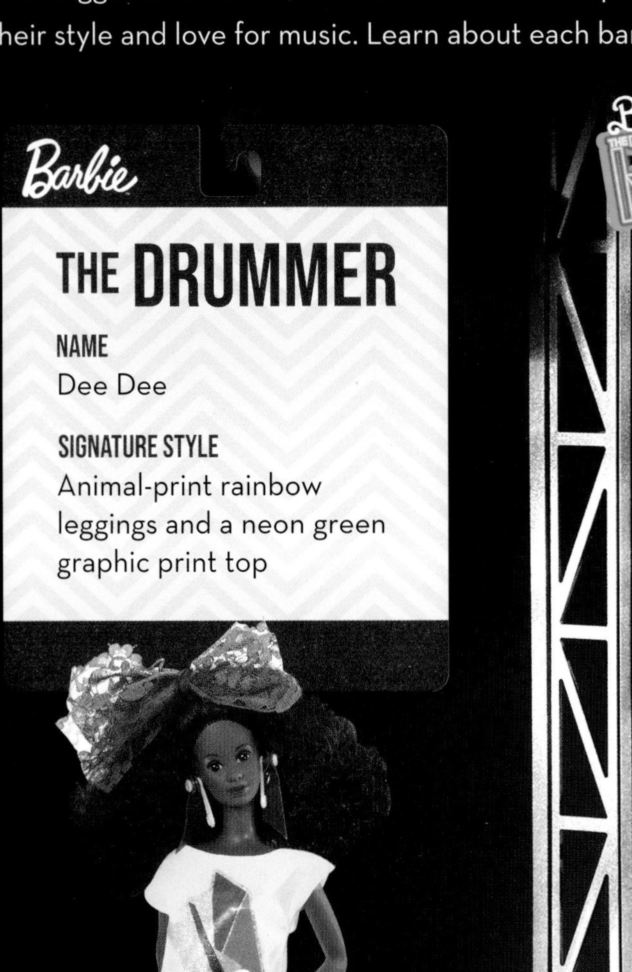

Barbie

THE DRUMMER

NAME
Dee Dee

SIGNATURE STYLE
Animal-print rainbow leggings and a neon green graphic print top

Barbie

THE SONGWRITER

NAME
Dana

SIGNATURE STYLE
White jacket with triangle graphics, blue leggings, and orange top

THE GUITARIST

NAME
Diva

SIGNATURE STYLE
Shiny blue jacket, purple pants, and neon yellow top

THE BACKUP SINGER

NAME
Derek

SIGNATURE STYLE
Multicolored jacket, black pleather pants, and pink cummerbund

THE LEAD SINGER

NAME
Barbie

SIGNATURE STYLE
Bright pink jacket, striped pink leggings, and silver top

MAJOR MOMENTS: 1990s
BRIEF HISTORY OF BARBIE HAIR

Barbie during the 1990s was totally about one thing—hair With the release of one of the best-selling Barbie dolls ever, Totally Hair™ Barbie was a major success.

NUMBER ONE

RELEASE YEAR
1959

HAIR HISTORY
The original Barbie hairstyle was a classic ponytail.

COLOR MAGIC™

RELEASE YEAR
1966

HAIR HISTORY
Color Magic™ Barbie had hair that could change color.

GROWIN' PRETTY HAIR BARBIE

RELEASE YEAR
1971

HAIR HISTORY
The hair length on th Barbie was retractab so it could be adjust to different lengths.

TOTALLY HAIR™ BARBIE

RELEASE YEAR 1992

SIGNATURE STYLE Pink, blue, white, and green graphic print dress with long sleeves

HAIR HISTORY The long, crimped hair on this Barbie doll was the longest hair she ever had.

BROOKLYN BARBIE

RELEASE YEAR 2021

SIGNATURE STYLE Black-and-white checkered shirt, denim skirt, and a pink fanny pack with pink jelly boots

MAKING HISTORY In 2021, Barbie Roberts from Brooklyn, New York, was introduced in the movie *Barbie Big City, Big Dreams*. She and Malibu Barbie met and became best friends at a music camp in New York City's Theater District.

FASHIONISTAS

One of the biggest moments in Barbie history came in 2016. For the first time, there were multiple Barbie body types released in the Fashionistas™ line. The 33 Fashionistas released in 2016 featured three new body types for Barbie—petite, tall, and curvy. See all 45 original Fashionistas in the next few pages!

1 STATEMENT STRIPES

RELEASE YEAR
2015

BODY TYPE
Original

SIGNATURE STYLE
Black-and-white shirt, black-and-white striped skirt, pink belt, necklace, purse, and platform shoes

2 DREAM FLORA

RELEASE YEAR
2015

BODY TYPE
Original

SIGNATURE STYLE
Pink shirt that says "Dream," pink floral skir and purse, an white heels

3 LA GIRL

RELEASE YEAR
2015

BODY TYPE
Original

SIGNATURE STYLE
Blue-and-white satin shirt that says "LA Girl," black leather skirt, lime green necklace and purse, and black sandals

4 DONUT DOTS

RELEASE YEAR
2015

BODY TYPE
Original

SIGNATURE STYLE
White shirt with six donuts, blue ruffled sk with white polka dots, blue sunglasses, and pink purse and heels

5 FLOWER FUN

RELEASE YEAR
2015

BODY TYPE
Original

SIGNATURE STYLE
Lime green shirt with black mesh and floral pattern, white denim skirt, pink hair clip and bracelet, off-white purse with fringe, and white heels

6 ROMPER CHIC

RELEASE YEAR
2015

BODY TYPE
Original

SIGNATURE STYLE
Pink patterned romper, blue over-the-shoulder purse, bronze earrings, and tan sandals

7 SPORTY STRIPES

RELEASE YEAR
2015

BODY TYPE
Original

SIGNATURE STYLE
Blue shirt with floral pattern and the number 09, black-and-white striped skirt, and pink purse and shoes

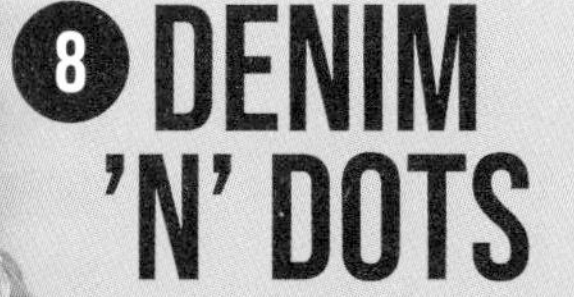

8 DENIM 'N' DOTS

RELEASE YEAR
2015

BODY TYPE
Original

SIGNATURE STYLE
Blue denim dress with white embellishments and black purse and boots

9 PLUM PLAID

RELEASE YEAR
2015

BODY TYPE
Original

SIGNATURE STYLE
White shirt, pink plaid skirt, gold necklace, pink purse, and black flats

10 KITTY DRESS

RELEASE YEAR
2015

BODY TYPE
Original

SIGNATURE STYLE
White-and-pink dress with kitten face that says "#Meow," gold necklace, blue purse, and black open-toed boots

11 RED RUFFLES

RELEASE YEAR
2015

BODY TYPE
Original

SIGNATURE STYLE
Red ruffled shirt, blue skirt with floral pattern, red heart-shaped purse, and blue heels

12 PANTS SO PIN

RELEASE YEAR
2015

BODY TYPE
Original

SIGNATURE STYLE
Fuzzy blue shirt, pink flor pants, clear purse, and white shoes

3 DOLLED UP DOTS

RELEASE YEAR
2016

BODY TYPE
Original

SIGNATURE STYLE
Pink skirt with black polka dots and white, green, and pink top with black polka dots

14 POWDER PINK

RELEASE YEAR
2016

BODY TYPE
Original

SIGNATURE STYLE
Baby doll dress with pink skirt, white top, and blue sash

15 SMILE WITH STYLE

RELEASE YEAR
2016

BODY TYPE
Original

SIGNATURE STYLE
Denim skirt with gray statement tee that says "Smile with Style," pink sandals, and necklace

16 GLAM TEAM

RELEASE YEAR
2016

BODY TYPE
Original

SIGNATURE STYLE
Shimmery blue tank dress with “Glam Team” and the number 84

17 ICE CREAM ROMPER

RELEASE YEAR
2016

BODY TYPE
Original

SIGNATURE STYLE
Blue-and-pink ice cream-print romper and blue glasses

18 VA-VA VIOLET

RELEASE YEAR
2016

BODY TYPE
Original

SIGNATURE STYLE
Blue skirt, black-and-white striped top, and statement necklace

19 RUBY RED FLORAL

RELEASE YEAR
2016

BODY TYPE
Original

SIGNATURE STYLE
Red skirt with black print and collared top

20 FANCY FLOWERS

RELEASE YEAR
2016

BODY TYPE
Original

SIGNATURE STYLE
Yellow floral sundress and blue platform heels

21 PRETTY IN PYTHON

RELEASE YEAR
2016

BODY TYPE
Original

SIGNATURE STYLE
Off-the-shoulder pink python print dress and necklace

22 CHAMBRAY CHIC

RELEASE YEAR
2016

BODY TYPE
Curvy

SIGNATURE STYLE
Chambray denim top, yellow skirt, and pink belt

23 LOVE THAT LACE

RELEASE YEAR
2016

BODY TYPE
Petite

SIGNATURE STYLE
Shiny red skirt knee-high boots, and long-sleeved white lace top

24 CRAZY FOR CORAL

RELEASE YEAR
2016

BODY TYPE
Petite

SIGNATURE STYLE
Halter dress with black top and pink-and-gold hi-low skirt

25 BLUE BROCADE

RELEASE YEAR
2016

BODY TYPE
Petite

SIGNATURE STYLE
Black-and-blue brocade print dress and black booties

26 SPRING INTO STYLE

RELEASE YEAR
2016

BODY TYPE
Curvy

SIGNATURE STYLE
Dress with floral print skirt and solid pink ruffle top

27 SWEETHEART STRIPES

RELEASE YEAR
2016

BODY TYPE
Curvy

SIGNATURE STYLE
Black-and-white striped top with black patent leather peplum and denim pencil skirt

28 FLORAL FLAIR

RELEASE YEAR
2016

BODY TYPE
Tall

SIGNATURE STYLE
Purple-and-pink dress with floral print

29 TERRIFIC TEAL

RELEASE YEAR
2016

BODY TYPE
Tall

SIGNATURE STYLE
Teal skirt and white, pink, and teal plaid top

30 WHITE & PINK PIZZAZZ

RELEASE YEAR
2016

BODY TYPE
Tall

SIGNATURE STYLE
Mesh white skirt and white-and-pink houndstooth print top

31 ROCK 'N' ROL PLAID

RELEASE YEAR
2016

BODY TYPE
Petite

SIGNATURE STYLE
Red, cream, and black plai skirt and “Roc n' Roll” white statement tee

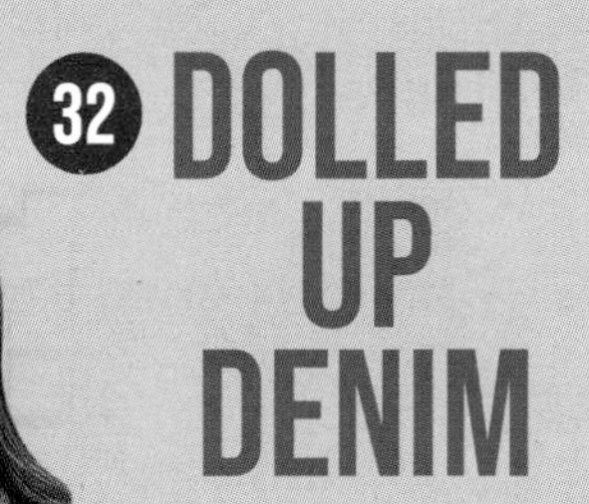

32 DOLLED UP DENIM

RELEASE YEAR
2016

BODY TYPE
Curvy

SIGNATURE STYLE
White lace top and denim dress, red statement necklace and matching shoes

33 FAB FRINGE

RELEASE YEAR
2016

BODY TYPE
Tall

SIGNATURE STYLE
Floral print black top and denim fringe shorts

34 B-FABULOUS

RELEASE YEAR
2016

BODY TYPE
Original

SIGNATURE STYLE
Yellow pleated skirt and teal triangle print graphic top

35 PEACE & LOVE

RELEASE YEAR
2016

BODY TYPE
Original

SIGNATURE STYLE
Pink top with black animal print and yellow peace sign, denim skirt, pink boots, and yellow purse

36 CHIC WITH A WINK

RELEASE YEAR
2016

BODY TYPE
Original

SIGNATURE STYLE
Long-sleeved pink-and-gray ombré top and pink, gray, and black plaid skirt

37 EVERYDAY CHIC

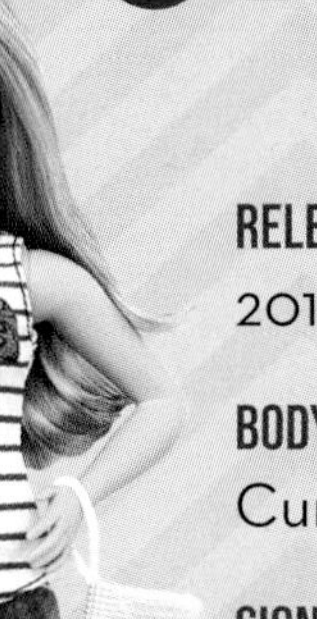

RELEASE YEAR
2016

BODY TYPE
Curvy

SIGNATURE STYLE
Pink-and-white striped top with black lace graphic bow and jeans with distressed detailing

38 SO SPORTY

RELEASE YEAR
2016

BODY TYPE
Curvy

SIGNATURE STYLE
Blue mesh fabric dress and black hat

39 EMOJI FUN

RELEASE YEAR
2016

BODY TYPE
Curvy

SIGNATURE STYLE
Emoji print denim vest, black skirt, and yellow top

40 PIZZA PIZZAZZ

RELEASE YEAR
2016

BODY TYPE
Petite

SIGNATURE STYLE
Red skirt, pink top with white triangle print, and black fedora

41 PRETTY IN PAISLEY

RELEASE YEAR
2016

BODY TYPE
Petite

SIGNATURE STYLE
Denim pencil skirt and teal-and-red paisley print top

42 BLUE VIOLET

RELEASE YEAR
2016

BODY TYPE
Petite

SIGNATURE STYLE
Denim shorts, pink tights, and bow print white shirt

43 LACEY BLUE

RELEASE YEAR
2016

BODY TYPE
Tall

SIGNATURE STYLE
Blue dress with graphic lace print, pink over-the-shoulder purse, and blue sunglasses

44 LEATHER & RUFFLES

RELEASE YEAR
2016

BODY TYPE
Tall

SIGNATURE STYLE
Blush ruffle skirt, gray top, and black leather vest

45 BOHO FRINGE

RELEASE YEAR
2016

BODY TYPE
Tall

SIGNATURE STYLE
Blue, red, and pink print dress and pink fringe purse

A year later it was Ken's turn to get a new look. In 2017, Ken got two new body types—broad and slim—eight hair colors, seven skin tones, and nine hairstyles, including a man bun and cornrows. There were 15 Ken dolls in the original release. Check out a selection of the original Ken Fashionistas dolls here!

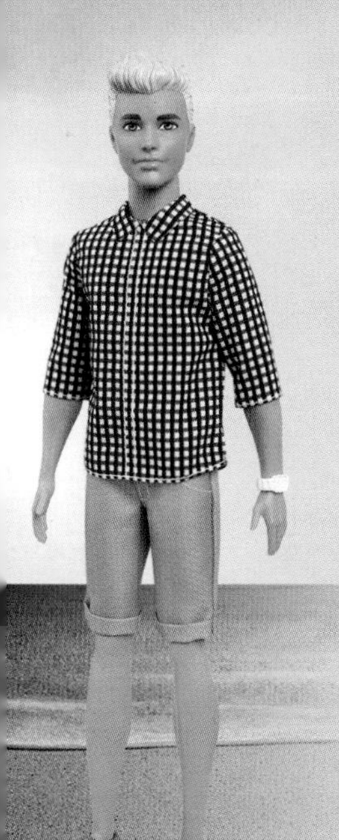

PREPPY CHECK

RELEASE YEAR
2017

BODY TYPE
Original

SIGNATURE STYLE
Long-sleeved white-and-blue checkered top and khaki cuffed shorts

CHILL IN CHECK

RELEASE YEAR
2017

BODY TYPE
Broad

SIGNATURE STYLE
Black denim pants and yellow-and-black plaid short-sleeved top

CLASSIC COOL

RELEASE YEAR
2017

BODY TYPE
Original

SIGNATURE STYLE
Dark gray pants, white short-sleeved top, and black tie

PLAID ON POINT

RELEASE YEAR
2017

BODY TYPE
Slim

SIGNATURE STYLE
Black jeans and red, black, and white plaid short-sleeved top

DISTRESSED DENIM

ELEASE YEAR

017

DY TYPE

road

GNATURE STYLE

istressed denim
horts and blue tribal
rint short-sleeved shirt

HYPED ON STRIPES

RELEASE YEAR

2017

BODY TYPE

Slim

SIGNATURE STYLE

Faded denim pants and striped pink, orange, yellow, and white tank

BLACK & WHITE

RELEASE YEAR

2017

BODY TYPE

Original

SIGNATURE STYLE

Black top with white polka dots and dark red pants

Now the Fashionistas line is more diverse than ever, featuring over 176 dolls, nine body types, 35 skin tones, and over 94 hairstyles between Barbie and Ken. With a focus on reflecting the world today, Fashionistas showcase different hair textures, skin features, and differently abled bodies. The storytelling possibilitie are endless!

119 RELEASE YEAR
2019

BODY TYPE
Original

SIGNATURE STYLE
Floral print striped shirtdress with front tie and cowboy boots

120 RELEASE YEAR
2019

BODY TYPE
Original

SIGNATURE STYLE
Colorful shimmery striped skirt and white tank top that says "Dream All Day"

121 RELEASE YEAR
2019

BODY TYPE
Limb differenc wearing a prosthetic leg

SIGNATURE STYLE
Blue dress wit ruffled sleeves and chevron print

122 **RELEASE YEAR**
2019

BODY TYPE
Tall

SIGNATURE STYLE
White graphic T-shirt with rainbow design and denim skirt

123 **RELEASE YEAR**
2019

BODY TYPE
Tall

SIGNATURE STYLE
Red pleather skirt with ruffle and black top with motorcycle graphic and the words "girl power"

124 **RELEASE YEAR**
2019

BODY TYPE
Petite

SIGNATURE STYLE
Denim overalls with white polka dots and white sleeveless top

125 **RELEASE YEAR**
2019

BODY TYPE
Curvy

SIGNATURE STYLE
Shiny short-sleeved floral print dress

126 **RELEASE YEAR**
2019

BODY TYPE
Curvy

SIGNATURE STYLE
Strapless yellow floral dress with front tie and bodice cutout

127 **RELEASE YEAR**
2019

BODY TYPE
Curvy

SIGNATURE STYLE
Purple dress with "Unicorn Believer" graphic and pink and teal mismatched sleeves

128 **RELEASE YEAR**
2019

BODY TYPE
Smaller bust

SIGNATURE STYLE
Pink camo graphic tank that says "Good Vibes Only" and denim shorts

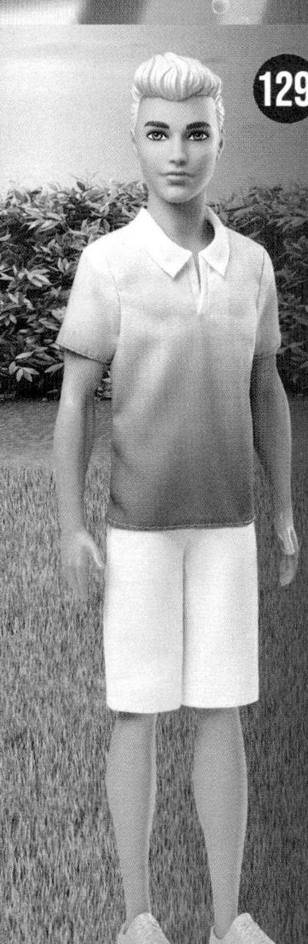

129 **RELEASE YEAR**
2019

BODY TYPE
Original

SIGNATURE STYLE
Blue ombré collared shirt and white shorts

30 **RELEASE YEAR**
2019

BODY TYPE
Slim

SIGNATURE STYLE
Faded jeans and mesh T-shirt featuring the number 4

131 **RELEASE YEAR**
2019

BODY TYPE
Broad

SIGNATURE STYLE
Gray sweatpant shorts and yellow sleeveless hoodie with "New York" graphic

132 **RELEASE YEAR**
2019

BODY TYPE
Original in wheelchair

SIGNATURE STYLE
Faded denim jeans and striped top with cutout shoulders

133 RELEASE YEAR
2019

BODY TYPE
Original in wheelchair

SIGNATURE STYLE
Faded denim jeans and striped top with cutout shoulders

134 RELEASE YEAR
2020

BODY TYPE
Original

SIGNATURE STYLE
Dress with cutouts, bows, and black-and-white polka dots in varying sizes

135 RELEASE YEAR
2020

BODY TYPE
More petite with vitiligo

SIGNATURE STYLE
Pink, white, black, and yellow striped maxi dress and black fanny pack

136 RELEASE YEAR
2020

BODY TYPE
Curvy

SIGNATURE STYLE
Light pink long-sleeved sweatshirt dress that says "Dream Often"

137 **RELEASE YEAR**
2020

BODY TYPE
Smaller bust and freckles

SIGNATURE STYLE
Color-blocked short-sleeved plaid dress with purple, red, and blue sections

138 **RELEASE YEAR**
2020

BODY TYPE
Original

SIGNATURE STYLE
Cuffed dark denim jeans and tie-dye tank top

139 **RELEASE YEAR**
2020

BODY TYPE
Original

SIGNATURE STYLE
Faded denim shorts and collared yellow graphic print shirt

Studio Fun International
An imprint of Printers Row Publishing Group
A division of Readerlink Distribution Services, LLC
9717 Pacific Heights Blvd, San Diego, CA 92121
www.studiofun.com

All notations of errors or omissions should be addressed to Studio Fun International, Editorial Department, at the above address.

ISBN: 978-0-7944-4718-2
Manufactured, printed, and assembled in Shaoguan, China.
Second printing, August 2022. SL/08/22
26 25 24 23 22 2 3 4 5 6

BARBIE FAS
Smile
WITH
Style
84

E BARBIE

Barbie® and Ken®
HE'S A DOLL!
TEEN-AGE FASHION MODEL
BARBIE'S BOYFRIEND
MATTEL, INC. TOYMAKERS
Barbie

Barbie
TEEN-AGE FASHION MODEL
MATTEL
INTERNATIONAL

VINTAG

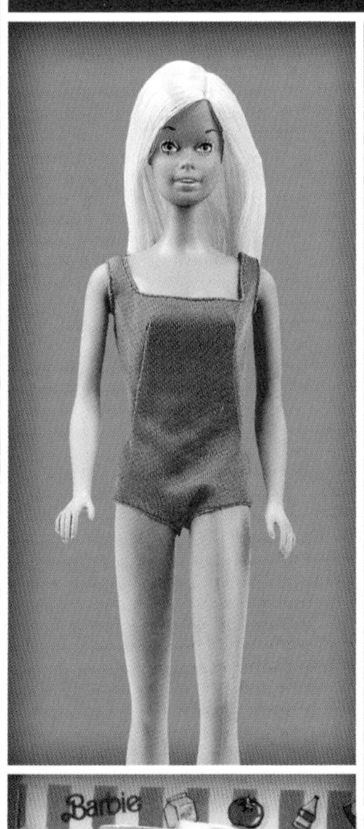

SHIONISTAS